Printed in the U.S.A.

ISBN 0-7172-8301-1

JIM HENSON'S MUPPETS

IN

Win Some, Lose Some

A Book About Sportsmanship

By Andrew Gutelle • Illustrated by Tom Brannon

GROLIER

"Hey, Kermit," shouted Fozzie. "Watch this!"

Fozzie and Piggy stood side by side at the far end of the basketball court.

"Ready, set, go!" shouted Piggy.

Fozzie and Piggy dashed down the court, passing the ball as they ran. When they reached the basketball hoop, Piggy flipped it into the air. The ball sailed into the basket. "Great shot," cheered Kermit.

Fozzie's basketball was a gift from his aunt Minnie. Since it had arrived, the three friends had played almost every day.

At first, when Fozzie had dribbled the ball, it had bounced off his foot. Piggy's shots had clanked against the rim of the basket, and Kermit's passes had landed in the flower bed.

But Kermit, Fozzie, and Piggy loved playing basketball. And slowly they learned to dribble, pass, and shoot a little better.

One Saturday as they were playing in the
the park, the basketball bounced away from
Piggy. She ran after it, but before she
reached the ball, a boy stuck out his foot and
stopped it from rolling. He picked it up and
flipped a behind-the-back pass to Piggy.
    "Wow!" she said.

"You guys are pretty good," said the boy.

"We are?" said Fozzie.

"My name is Kevin," he said. "My family just moved to town, and I haven't met anyone yet. Can I play basketball with you?"

"Sure!" said Kermit.

"I have an idea," Kevin continued. "Instead of just shooting the ball, why don't we play a game?"

"We've never played a real game," Kermit replied. "We just play for fun."

"But a real game *will* be fun," Kevin said.

Piggy, Kermit, and Fozzie agreed to play. Kevin picked Fozzie to be on his team. Before the game began, Kevin explained the rules:

"There are two players on each team. Each basket counts as one point. The first team to make ten baskets is the winner."

When the game began, Kevin and Fozzie had the ball first. Fozzie dashed to his favorite place right under the basket. He waited for Kevin to pass the ball to him, but Kevin ignored Fozzie. Instead, he shot the ball and scored the basket himself.

Kevin kept doing everything he could think of to win. He took all the shots, hogged the ball, and passed to Fozzie as little as possible. He cheered when Piggy missed a shot and shoved Kermit out of the way to get to the ball first.

Kevin loved winning. His team won that game and every other one the kids played during the week.

Fozzie, Kermit, and Piggy tried to play the way they always had. But the more they worried about playing well, the worse they did.

The next Saturday, Kermit, Fozzie, and Piggy stopped for lunch on their way to the park. After ordering three slices of pizza, they talked about their problem.

"Playing basketball with Kevin is no fun at all," said Fozzie.

"I know," agreed Kermit.

"I want to tell him to stop being such a bad sport," added Piggy. "But he wants to win so badly, I know he won't listen."

"Maybe we can't change Kevin, but we can make sure he doesn't change us," suggested Kermit. "Let's try to play for fun, the way we used to."

When the three friends arrived at the basketball court, Kevin was waiting for them. It was Fozzie's turn to be his team-mate.

The game started badly. Right away, Fozzie dribbled the ball off his own foot, and it went out of bounds. Kevin glared angrily at him, but Kermit patted Fozzie on the back.

"Good try, Fozzie!" shouted Piggy.

As the game continued, Fozzie, Piggy, and Kermit cheered each other on—even though they weren't all on the same team. Playing basketball became fun again. Kermit and Piggy played so well that they tied the score. There was just one basket to go.

Kevin held the ball. Fozzie stood near the basket waiting for a pass, but Kevin ignored him. He dribbled past Kermit, jumped, and shot. The ball hit the rim and bounced out. Kevin had missed!

Piggy grabbed the ball, shot, and scored. She and Kermit had won!

"Nice shot, Piggy," said Fozzie.

"You're lucky I missed," said Kevin. "I *always* make that shot, and if I had, we would have won the game!"

"Try not to get so upset," said Kermit. "Even good players lose once in a while."

"Well, I shouldn't have," insisted Kevin. "Let's play again—same teams. This time I'll beat you."

The new game began. At first, Kevin scored lots of baskets, but working together, Piggy and Kermit began to catch up. Finally, Piggy made a basket to tie the score. One more basket would win the game.

Fozzie held the ball. As Kevin dashed to the basket, Fozzie threw a perfect pass to him. Kevin caught it and carefully shot it. The ball rolled around the rim and then fell out. Kevin had missed again!

Kermit scooped up the ball and scored. He and Piggy had won a second time.

Kevin stood there, stunned. "That was the easiest shot I had all game—and I missed it," he said sadly.

Fozzie walked over to him. "Nice game," he said, patting Kevin on the back.

Kevin was amazed. "You're not mad at me? But I lost the game for us."

"I know you did the best you could," said Fozzie. "That's what matters."

"In my old neighborhood," said Kevin quietly, "kids weren't so nice when you lost."

"Around here, winning isn't so important," explained Piggy. "Being a good sport—and having fun with your friends—is what really counts."

Kevin thought for a minute. "You know, you're right," he admitted.

Kermit tossed the ball to Kevin. "Why don't we shoot some more baskets together?"

Kevin's face brightened. "Okay," he said, tossing the ball back to Kermit. "But this time, why don't *you* go first?"

Let's Talk About Sportsmanship

There's an old saying that goes: "It's not whether you win or lose, it's how you play the game." But Kevin didn't know that. He wanted to win so badly, he forgot to be a good sport. His new friends showed him that winning is not the most important thing in the world. To Kermit, Piggy, and Fozzie, having fun playing together was more important than winning.

Here are some questions about sportsmanship for you to think about:

Have you ever lost a game that you really wanted to win? How did you feel? How did you act? How did the person who won act?

Have you ever won an important game? How did that make you feel? Did you think about the person who lost?